Chapter One

Tara yawned and stretched, then smiled when she remembered she didn't have to get up yet. It was the first day of the summer holidays. She thought about all the fun things she was going to do with her friends. She was most excited about her eleventh birthday in a couple of weeks, and the party she was having to celebrate. The sun was already streaming brightly through a gap in her pale blue curtains and she was too hot under the bedcovers. It was going to be a beautiful day – perfect for practising gymnastics in the garden.

Tara loved gym. A year and a half ago, when she was in Year Five at school, her class had learned to do handstands and cartwheels in their PE lessons. As soon as she kicked her legs up into her first wobbly handstand, she was hooked. She'd always loved watching gymnastics on TV, but actually doing it was even better. So she spent every spare moment practising – out in the garden at weekends, in the living room or her bedroom if it was raining. Now she had the whole summer holidays stretching out before her and she was going to use every single day to work on her skills.

She closed her eyes, listening to the birds outside, and thought about all the things she was going to learn. A backward walkover was top of her list. She was nearly there, so close that sometimes when she was practising she felt like she was sure to manage it if she just tried once more. There were so many other things she wanted to learn too – like backflips and somersaults – but she knew she wouldn't achieve them all this summer. Everything in gymnastics took a long time and a lot of work.

She threw back the covers, suddenly wanting to get started right away. Downstairs, her six-year-old sister Anna was already up and watching cartoons, with a half-eaten bowl of cereal on her lap. Dad had gone to work and Mum was nowhere to be seen. She was probably enjoying the first day of not having to take Tara and Anna to school.

"Morning," said Tara, helping herself to some cereal.

Anna mumbled something, but Tara couldn't hear what it was because Anna had her spoon in her mouth. Tara ate her breakfast, washed it down with juice, and then ran back upstairs to get dressed. A T-shirt and shorts were all she needed for practising gym, so she was soon running back down the stairs, pulling her blonde hair up into a messy ponytail as she went.

The garden was sunny and warm. She was glad to feel a little breeze on her arms and face – gymnastics was hard work and it was even tougher when it was boiling hot outside. Tara's garden was quite big. A rectangle of grass took up most of the space, which was brilliant for practising floor routines and taking a run-up for round-offs and handsprings. There were flower beds around three sides, and the fourth side, nearest the house, had a little concrete patio they used for barbecues.

She did a quick warm-up in the middle of the garden. Warming up was really important; they were always told that in PE at school. She definitely didn't want to pull any muscles – the idea of an injury stopping her from practising all summer was too horrible to think about! Secretly, Tara also liked warming up properly because it made her feel like a serious gymnast. Real gymnasts like Beth Tweddle and Shawn Johnson had to warm up well because they did such difficult things, and Tara wanted to be just like them. She swung her arms around in big circles and stretched her leg muscles by lunging forward, and to the side. Then she bent to touch her toes and, keeping her legs straight, put her hands flat on the floor, feeling the stretch down the back of her legs.

With her warm-up done, she got started on the day's work. She practised easy things first, as a kind of extension of the warm-up. Cartwheels and round-offs; bridges and handstands and splits. These were all things she'd learned to do last summer. When she was in Year Five, there had been a girl in the year above who did gymnastics at a club outside school, and she'd shown Tara how to do some of these moves. They came naturally to her now. The more tricky ones came next. These were mostly things she'd seen the older girl doing and had taught herself later, when she was able to do the basics. She practised moving from a handstand into a bridge position, and then pushed her hands off the floor so that she stood up. It had taken her every weekend of the summer term to learn that and she was very proud of it.

She stood in the middle of the garden, wishing that today might be the day she did her first backward walkover. She was already part of the way there. She could stand with her feet apart and bend over backwards into a bridge. Then she kicked her legs over so that she was standing again. It had taken her ages and ages to manage that last bit. She'd started by doing it with her feet up on the sofa or her bed, and when she could do that she'd used a sturdy box that Anna stood on to see into the bathroom mirror when she brushed her teeth. Anna called it the Grow-Tall-Step, and she'd cried when Tara left it outside overnight. That was when Tara decided it was time to try kicking over just from the ground. It was hard. It had taken days and days of aching wrists, a sore back and disappointed hopes. But she'd got there. Now she could do it, easy-peasy, and that made all the work feel worthwhile. It was time she moved on to real walkovers.

She stood with one foot pointed out in front of her and her arms stretched up. She bent backwards smoothly, raising her leg as she went so that she ended up in a bridge with one leg pointing up to the clear blue sky. She pushed hard with the foot that was still on the ground, but she couldn't do it – she couldn't kick her leg over to standing position. Instead, her feet landed back in a bridge. She let her body slump to the ground. For a moment, she lay on her back, one hand shielding her eyes from the bright sun.

"Come on, Tara," she whispered. "You didn't expect to do it first time, did you? Try again." She rolled over and got to her feet. Sometimes it was tempting to give up. But then she'd remember gymnasts she'd seen on TV, and the things the girl at school had been able to do, and she kept trying. She wanted to be like those gymnasts more than anything in the world.

She gave the backward walkover another try. The same thing happened. Again. And again. And again. It was hard but she knew this was how gymnastics worked. All of this would be worth it when she finally managed to do a real walkover.

"Tara!" Anna's voice broke into her concentration just as she was about to have another go. "Mum says you've got to come and have lunch!"

Lunch? Tara was shocked. Was it really lunchtime already? She'd been so focused she hadn't noticed the sun travelling across the sky, or the day getting hotter.

"Mu-um," Tara said slowly, while she ate her sandwich.

"Yes, Tara?"

"You said we'd talk about it again in the summer, and it's summer now...so...can I go to a gym club?"

"We'll see," replied Mum. "We'll have to find out about the ones near here."

"Please?" begged Tara. She'd been pestering Mum and Dad for ages now, and Mum knew that Tara had already gone on the internet and looked up all about the local clubs. The real problem, Tara knew, was that Mum was worried she'd get bored of gymnastics. But there was no chance of that! She just *had* to make her parents see that.

In the afternoon, Tara pretended that the soft green grass was the blue square of a gymnastics floor area. She danced and jumped and twirled, scattering her favourite skills through the routine as she went. She was imagining elegant music in her head, with a good rhythm for tumbling. She couldn't do any really good tumbling runs yet, not like the gymnasts she saw on TV – they all did backflips and somersaults with loads of twists and turns. But Tara still managed to put together a few tumbling sequences – on diagonal lines across the floor, just like world-class gymnasts did – with round-offs, one-handed cartwheels and her best skill of all: a handspring. She'd only just learned to do those, and she still needed a bit of a run-up, so she put one right at the end of her routine. A couple more run-throughs and she was ready to perform.

She stood in one corner of her floor area. In her mind, her T-shirt and shorts became a gorgeous blue and black leotard, and all around the flower beds, the crowd were waiting for her to compete. She stepped forward, and raised her arms to present herself to the judges by the washing line. Then she took up her starting position, and the music swelled around her as she began the routine. She danced expressively, she finished every move as neatly as possible; she jumped and balanced and pretended that she was Beth Tweddle, one of her favourite gymnasts.

Tara was nearing the end of her routine and it was time for the handspring. She took a deep breath, pointed her foot and ran diagonally across the floor. She launched herself forwards onto her hands and sprang over onto her feet. She landed in a squat position, which wasn't how it was supposed to be, but it was the best she could do so far. She stretched, did a few more turns and leaps, and finished the routine with a graceful pose. Her imaginary crowd went wild, and she was just wondering what her score would be when she realized that the clapping was real.

"Good job, Tara!" said Dad. Tara went red. She hadn't noticed that she'd actually had a proper audience!

Later that evening, Tara lay on her bed and watched the World Championships from last year, which she'd recorded when it was on TV. She'd watched it a hundred times since then, maybe more, and she knew all the gymnasts' routines by heart. Her favourite routines were the ones on the floor. Would she ever get a chance to do those things? Some things were easy enough to practise in the garden, but she'd need big, squashy safety mats to try anything really difficult. Even if she had mats, she didn't have anyone to show her how to do the moves. Would she ever know what it felt like to twist through the air in a somersault? *No chance*, she thought. She sighed, and rewound her favourite floor routine again. She imitated some of the gymnast's graceful arm movements while she lay on her bed. Even if she did nothing else all summer, she *would* show Mum and Dad that gymnastics was not just a passing phase. It was the only thing she ever wanted to do.

Chapter Two

Tara kicked her legs up into a handstand, walked her hands forward three times, and then had to come down. She went up again. Walking on her hands was addictive! This time she managed four steps before she lost her balance and came down, her legs twisting to the side.

"Watch out!" laughed Kate, one of her two best friends. Her other friend, Emily, laughed too.

"Don't you ever get bored of doing that?" she asked.

Tara shook her head and strands of blonde hair whipped across her eyes. She pushed them behind her ears and sat down on the grass with her friends. They were in Kate's garden, enjoying the lovely sunshine and the fact that they didn't have to go back to school for six whole weeks. They'd been there most of the day, chatting and listening to music on Kate's iPod, which she had plugged into some speakers.

"I love this song!" said Kate. She started to nod her head and move her arms in time to the music, dancing as well as she could while sitting down.

"Nice moves, Kate," Tara giggled. "You should have performed that at the leavers' show." Kate went to a dance class once a week. Year Six had performed a talent show in their last week at Meadow Lane Junior School, and Kate had tried to get Tara and Emily to do a dance with her. Emily had been too shy, and in the end Tara and Kate had left it too late to make anything up. Some of the other girls in their class did dances, but Tara thought Kate would probably have been better than all of them. She was definitely more confident than anyone else.

Kate pretended to be annoyed and narrowed her eyes at Tara. "Bet you can't do any better."

Tara grinned at her and jumped up. She listened to the rhythm of the music for a few seconds, and then she started dancing. She made it up as she went along, jumping, twirling, and trying the kind of dance steps she'd seen her favourite girl bands doing. She grabbed Emily's hand and dragged her up, trying to get her to dance too, but Emily didn't really know what to do. Tara took her friend's hands and started to spin around, faster and faster, until they were both shrieking and laughing. Emily let go and they stumbled away from each other.

"That's not dancing," scoffed Kate, standing up. "*I'll* show you some real dancing." She started to make up her own dance to the song, which was nearly over by then.

"Ooh, that was cool!" said Emily. "Show me how you did that last bit?"

Kate did it again, flicking her arm out to the side, then jumping into a half-turn. Emily tried to copy, but she kept getting her arms in the wrong place.

"What did you do before the arm thing?" Tara asked suddenly. Kate showed her the little dance again, and she followed it as well as she could.

"Put that song back on," said Kate.

Tara sorted out the music, and then Kate went straight into the same short sequence of steps.

"Do it slower!" begged Emily. Kate took a deep breath and shook her long, dark hair back over her shoulders.

"Come over here, Tara," she ordered. "I can't show you both if you're doing handstands into the flower beds." Tara and Emily exchanged smiles – Kate loved being in charge. Tara went and stood next to Emily as instructed. "Start with your right leg," Kate said, and turned around so that they could copy her as she danced…

When they'd got the hang of it, Kate started to add more moves. Tara and Emily threw in ideas too and by the end of the afternoon they had a dance long enough to last the whole song.

"Shall we perform it for our mums when they come to pick us up?" suggested Emily.

"Good idea," said Tara.

"Or…" Kate began, and they could see in her eyes that she was coming up with something that she thought would be even better. "We could make up some more dances and do a show for them in a few weeks!"

"We could do solos as well as stuff together," said Tara, knowing that her friends wouldn't want to put any gymnastics into the group dances.

"Definitely," Kate nodded, but Emily looked worried. "I'll help you with yours, Em, if you want," she offered.

"Thanks," Emily sighed.

Tara was lost in her own thoughts. She couldn't wait to get started on her solo. She'd find some perfect music, maybe something like the classical pieces gymnasts used in big competitions. Then she'd make up a brilliant routine to show off all the new skills she'd learned. As the show was a few weeks away, maybe she'd even be able to include a backward walkover.

Chapter Three

Tara woke up the next morning to the sound of Anna screaming her name. She jumped out of bed and ran down the stairs, wondering what was wrong.

"Come quickly, come quickly!" yelled Anna.

"What is it?" Tara asked breathlessly, crashing through the living room door. Anna was in her usual place on the floor in front of the TV, a bowl of cereal in her lap.

Gym Stars

"Are you okay?" Tara demanded.

"Look," said Anna, pointing her spoon at the TV. Tara looked. Anna was watching one of the Saturday morning TV shows where the presenters ran competitions and games, and had singers and film stars on to talk about their latest hits. On the screen, one of the presenters was chatting to a group of boys and girls. "They're gymnasts," Anna told her. "Like you."

Tara sat on the sofa. She'd missed most of the interview – the gymnasts were now going over to a floor area that had been specially set out for them. Loud, dramatic music started up and the gymnasts began a spectacular routine. It was like nothing Tara had ever seen before – instead of performing individually, the gymnasts worked in pairs and groups of three and four, lifting each other up into high balances, and throwing the tiniest girls and boys into the air, where they somersaulted round and round before they were caught again by the taller gymnasts on the floor.

It was incredible! Anna had said they were like Tara, but she knew she would never be able to do any of those things, not if she trained for a million years. The routine was over too quickly for Tara. She made a mental note to find it on the internet later. Then she could replay it again and again until she knew it by heart.

"That's all we've got time for this morning," said the presenter with a grin, while the gymnasts smiled and caught their breath in the background. "Good luck in the competition, guys!" He turned to the gymnasts and gave them a big thumbs up, and then the show was over. Tara was still staring at the TV, but she didn't see the adverts that were now playing. In her head, she was watching the gymnasts' routine again, trying to remember everything they'd done. It made her even more determined to keep practising. She glanced out of the window and then slumped back onto the sofa immediately – she'd been so caught up in the gymnastics on TV that she hadn't even noticed raindrops streaking down the windows. There would be no gymnastics in the garden today.

After breakfast, she went up to her room and got dressed. What could she do now? she wondered, sitting on her bed. She was itching to start working on her routine for the show with Kate and Emily – she'd chosen some music the night before and she could already see the routine taking shape in her head. But there wasn't space in her bedroom to work out a whole routine. At least she could work on her backward walkovers – that was just as important as making up the routine itself.

She tried to be quiet, but it really was impossible. Every time she tried to get all the way over, her legs came crashing down to the floor again. Dad was reading the newspaper downstairs and she knew he'd be getting annoyed – but this was *important*. She decided she'd just have five more tries, and then she'd give up for the day... And that was when it happened. She stood neatly, bent backwards and lifted her leg, pushed off the floor with her other foot, and smoothly brought her legs over to land behind her hands. She'd done it!

"YES!" she yelled. She jumped up in the air with her fists raised in triumph.

There was thunder on the stairs.

"*What* is going on in here?" shouted Dad, pushing Tara's bedroom door open. "It sounds like you've got a herd of elephants thumping around."

"Sorry," Tara replied. She tried to look apologetic, but she couldn't stop smiling. She'd finally done a real backward walkover!

"You've got the garden for gymnastics," said Dad. "You don't need to do it in here as well."

"But it's raining," Tara protested.

Dad opened his mouth and then stopped. He was thinking about something. "Come downstairs," he said at last. "I've got something to show you."

Tara followed him down the stairs and into the

living room. He picked something up from the little table in the corner.

"I got this for you this morning," he said. He handed her a pale blue leaflet with a drawing of a gymnast at the top. "Thought you might be interested."

Tara looked at Dad for a moment before glancing down at the leaflet in her hand. Her eyes widened as she read the front page. Under the gymnast it said *Silverdale Gymnastics Club*, and below that, *Summer Gymnastics Camp*. She'd known about Silverdale almost her whole life. Every year, as part of the town summer fête, she and her friends went to Silverdale to watch the gym club's Summer Display. It was always the highlight of the day for Tara; gymnasts of all ages and abilities performed routines for the town. Some of them were amazing, while some were groups of beginners – girls and boys like her. She had spent hours and hours daydreaming about being a Silverdale gymnast.

"How about it?" Dad asked with a grin.

"Can I go?" Tara whispered. "Please?"

"I think you'll have to," said Dad. "It's the only way I'll ever get any peace."

Tara looked at the leaflet again. The camp was only for a week, but that was better than nothing. She threw her arms around Dad. "Thank you, thank you, thank you!" she chanted.

A real gymnastics club! This was going to be the best summer of her life.

Chapter Four

Tara could think about nothing else that day. She kept asking Mum if she'd phoned Silverdale yet to book a place on the camp. Mum finally called the club later that afternoon and Tara hung around, listening to the conversation. She was worried that it would be booked up already. Luckily, there was a space left for her, and she immediately wrote GYM CAMP on her calendar in pink pen. It was on Monday!

Summertime and Somersaults

The next day, Mum took Tara and Anna shopping. Tara glanced in the window of the dance shop as they walked past. The shop was full of shoes for different types of dancing, and rails of bright and glittery leotards ran all around the walls. They sold gymnastics leotards too, which was why Tara always stared longingly at the window display. It had changed since she'd last seen it. As well as the usual pyramid of ballet shoes, there was a mannequin wearing a purple velvety leotard with silver sparkles on the shoulders. It was sleeveless and, with one arm stretched up, the mannequin looked like a perfect gymnast.

"Can we go in here?" Tara asked.

Mum looked at her watch. "Okay," she agreed. "But just a quick look. We still need to get you both some new trainers. I don't know what you do to them, but your old ones are falling apart!"

Playing netball and rounders and running round the playing field had caused that, thought

Tara. If they did gymnastics all year at school, it would always be bare feet and no one's trainers would get ruined.

Tara hurried into the shop, with Mum and Anna following behind.

"Good morning," said the shop assistant with a smile. "Can I help you with anything?"

"No thanks," Mum said firmly. "We're just having a look."

Tara wandered slowly around the room. She found the rail of gymnastics leotards and ran her fingers slowly over the soft velvet and silky lycra. She was starting the summer camp at Silverdale Gym Club tomorrow. She was going to need a leotard to wear. There was every colour she could think of here; some were long sleeved and some had no sleeves, like the one in the window. There were leotards with sparkly bits, ones with lots of different colours, and loads with patterns on. How would she ever be able to choose? Right in the middle of the rail was a black leotard. It was surrounded by so many bright colours and patterns that she almost didn't notice it. She pulled it out to see if it was just plain black, and discovered that tiny silver sparkles twisted in a fluttering ribbon shape from one shoulder all the way down to the opposite hip. She took it down from the rail and held it up in front of her. The sparkles looked like stars on a dark night. It was beautiful – a real medal-winning leotard. And it was even the right size.

"This is *boring*," Anna moaned. "You said we could go to The Disney Store."

"In a minute, Anna," said Mum. "Come on, Tara. We've got to get home soon."

"Mum, can I get a leotard for gym?" Tara asked, eagerly turning to Mum and showing her the black and silver one.

Mum sighed. "Not today," she said. "You're only going for a week."

"But what am I going to wear?" cried Tara.

"A T-shirt and shorts will be fine," Mum replied.

"No it won't," Tara muttered, putting the leotard back on the rail. She hoped it would still be there by the time she'd saved up enough money to buy it. Anna was already halfway out the door and Mum was hurrying to catch up with her. Tara dragged along behind them. It was so unfair. She was going to be the only one at Silverdale without a leotard, and the other gymnasts would think she was just playing around and not taking it seriously.

They'd only just got home when Emily and Kate arrived for the afternoon. Tara forgot about the leotard when she saw her friends, and the three girls ran out into the garden to talk about their dance show.

"How are you two getting on with your solos?" asked Kate.

"I haven't started mine yet," Tara admitted. "But I've got lots of ideas!"

"I tried…" said Emily. "I picked some music,

but I couldn't think of any good dance steps for it."

"I haven't done anything yet either," laughed Kate.

"Let's practise the group dance again," suggested Emily. "I think I've forgotten most of it."

Between them all they soon remembered everything they'd done before. They changed a few things as they went along, and practised until they were perfectly in time with each other. But Kate had forgotten her iPod, and it was difficult practising without a beat. After a while, they found themselves sprawled on the grass, chatting and linking daisies together in chains.

"What are we going to wear for the dance show?" Emily asked.

Tara thought of the leotard again. If she could save up enough to buy it in the next few weeks, she'd wear that for her solo routine. It was her birthday soon, and she might get money from Auntie Hazel, but she'd need to save her pocket money too. "Whatever we want for our solos," she said quickly.

Kate nodded. "But what about the group one?"

"Jeans and different coloured T-shirts?" suggested Emily.

Kate pulled a face. "Boring."

"What then?" asked Tara.

"I don't know. We could go shopping and find some matching things."

"Won't that be expensive?" Emily asked worriedly.

Tara didn't like that idea either. If she had to buy something to wear for the group dance, she wouldn't be able to get that beautiful leotard. "I bet we've already got loads of stuff the same as each other," she said. "Let's go and look in my wardrobe now."

"I've got a skirt like that," said Kate, pointing at a denim skirt hanging up in Tara's wardrobe. Tara pulled it out. "Actually," continued Kate, looking at it properly, "I think it's the same one."

"I've got one similar," added Emily.

Kate pulled out a light, summery top and held it up against herself, looking in the mirror. "This is really pretty," she said. "How come you never wear it?"

"Don't know." Tara shrugged. "It's a bit posh for just going shopping and stuff. You can borrow it if you want."

"Thanks," said Kate. "I think it would be too small for me though." She grinned at Tara, who was small for her age and sometimes got sick of people pointing out how short she was. "You should wear it for your birthday party next week!"

"Good idea," said Tara, taking the top from Kate. It was light pink with white flowers, and had a thin line of white lace along the bottom and at the edges of the short sleeves. She smiled widely, thinking about her birthday. She was excited about having a party in the garden with all her friends from school. Emily and Kate were going to sleep over afterwards, and they'd already planned which films they were going to watch, and games they could play without making too much noise in the middle of the night.

Kate had moved on to Tara's chest of drawers.

"What about this?" Tara suggested, spotting a dark pink fitted T-shirt that she'd forgotten about. "You've got something this colour, haven't you, Em?"

"Sort of," said Emily. "It's a bit lighter, but close enough."

Kate turned to look at the top. "I don't have anything like that," she said. Tara frowned and put the top back in her drawer.

"Wait," said Emily. "I've got two tops that are almost that colour. You can wear one of mine, Kate."

"Brilliant!" Kate smiled. She and Emily were roughly the same height and size so they often borrowed each other's clothes. Tara sometimes wished that she was the same – she could only share things like bags and scarves and bracelets.

"That was easy," said Emily, and Tara could tell she was glad they didn't need to buy anything new.

"Now the dance will look awesome," said Kate. Tara pictured the three of them dancing together in their matching outfits, and she definitely agreed. If only she could get that leotard, her solo routine would look just as great.

In bed that night, Tara could hardly sleep thinking about the next day and her first training session at a real gym club. She hoped the coach would be nice. She wondered how many people would be doing the course, whether they'd all be girls, and how old they would be. She started to worry that they'd all be much better than her. What if they'd all been doing gymnastics since they were really young? Some children started when they were three or four. She was nearly eleven, which meant she'd missed out on seven years already.

She squeezed her eyes shut to calm herself down. She wasn't a *complete* beginner. In her head, she went through a list of all the things she'd taught herself to do. She'd really got the hang of backward walkovers now, and she couldn't wait to try doing one on a real gymnastics floor. Smiling, she started to imagine wonderful things happening; things that she knew wouldn't come true, but couldn't help wishing for. Like, maybe she would learn to do a perfect front somersault or brilliant backflip.

Tomorrow she'd find out how she measured up against the others at Silverdale, but for tonight she let herself dream. And now that she was going to get a taste of proper training, maybe one day she really would be a world-class gymnast.

Chapter Five

The entrance lobby at Silverdale Gym Club was already packed full of children and parents when Tara and Mum arrived. There were a few coaches wandering around too, dressed in navy blue T-shirts that said Silverdale Gymnastics Club in white letters on the chest.

Tara looked around slowly, taking everything in. She was only coming to Silverdale for a week and she wanted to remember every detail. She'd been there to watch the Summer Display but it had been full of people then and she hadn't had much time to look around. The lobby was fairly small, with a corridor leading off on each side. Straight ahead were big double doors that stood open to reveal the gym. Tara stared through the doors, anticipation bubbling up inside her. Then she tore her gaze away, knowing that she'd get to see more of the gym later.

On the walls of the lobby there were rows and rows of framed photographs. She went closer to the nearest wall to get a better look. Some were photos of big groups of gymnasts in their own clothes, with their arms around each other. The labels under these ones said they were taken at training camps in other countries, and, looking again, she could see palm trees in the background of one photo, snow on the ground in another. Lots of the photos showed gymnasts with medals, trophies and bouquets of flowers. There were girls by themselves, boys by themselves, and quite a few pictures of groups of two, three or four gymnasts together. Other photos showed big groups of gymnasts in poses, and the labels on these all said *Summer Display* and the year they were from. Last year, while Tara sat watching the Silverdale display with Mum and Anna, she had wished she was part of the club. Now, for one week, she was.

Suddenly, Tara realized someone was talking to her.

"Can I take your name?" asked a woman with long black hair tied up into a swinging ponytail.

"Tara Bailey," Tara replied, and her voice came out much quieter than she'd expected.

"Nice to meet you, Tara." The coach smiled. "I'm Lucy. I'll be doing most of the coaching for the ten-to-fourteen year olds this week." She looked down at the clipboard she was holding. "You're ten, right? So you'll be in my group."

Tara nodded. "I'll be eleven on Saturday," she added.

"We'll all sing 'Happy Birthday' to you on Friday then!" Lucy said with a big smile. "Take your shoes and socks off," she continued, "and go and sit on the floor inside." Tara looked where the coach was pointing. Through the open doors she could see the blue floor area, which was filling up with all the other people here for the summer camp. She noticed the white line that marked the edge of the square – just like on the floors gymnasts used in big competitions on TV. Her feet itched to step onto it and try out a round-off – launching herself onto her hands into the beginning of a fast cartwheel, then springing out of it onto both feet at the same time.

"You can leave your bottle of water and anything else on this table," Lucy told her, pointing out a big table in the lobby that was quickly being piled with bags, bottles and lunch boxes. Then the coach went off to talk to another new arrival.

"Have a lovely day," said Mum, and gave her a kiss on the cheek.

Summertime and Somersaults

"Bye!" said Tara and she skipped away, a little embarrassed. Even if lots of the kids here were younger, she was going to be in the older group, and being kissed goodbye was *so* not cool. She found a space on the table for her things and went hesitantly into the gym.

Inside, the space was even bigger than she'd remembered from watching the display. The first thing she came to was the floor area, to the left of the doors. Tara's breath caught in her throat when she stepped forward onto it. The carpet was soft under her bare feet. Tara knew that a gymnastics floor area was often called a "sprung floor" because it was a bit bouncy, and she couldn't wait to try out something like a handspring – landings would be much better in here than in the garden! She looked around the rest of the gym. Next to the floor were two sets of asymmetric bars, and beside them were three beams. On the other side of the big gym was another floor area which was where the audience always sat for the Summer Display, and at the back there was a long blue track that led to a pit full of foam blocks, great for making landings softer. Tara saw an older girl run fast down the track and throw herself into a round-off and then up into a twisting somersault. Behind the tumbling track was another running track and the vault. At the very back of the gym were two trampolines, and another big foam pit. Above the foam blocks was a high bar, and Tara could see a boy swinging round and round in full circles.

There were gymnasts everywhere. A group of tiny girls were using the floor area on the other side of the gym. Their coach was helping them to do forward rolls. In their little pink leotards, Tara thought they looked very sweet, but she knew that they were getting a great head start on gymnastics. Maybe one of them would grow up to be a champion.

The air smelled a bit stale, and it was already quite warm, even though it was only 9.30 in the morning. Tara found a space on the floor near some girls who looked like they might be her age, and sat down. She was glad that almost everyone else was wearing a T-shirt and shorts, like her. She had to admit that Mum had been right after all.

The floor quickly filled up. With a bit of guessing, Tara counted fifteen who looked likely to be in the older group. There were about fifteen younger kids too. Then Lucy came in with three other coaches and introduced them. She and Greg would be coaching the ten-to-fourteen year olds, while Michelle and Amanda would work with the six-to-nine age group. They split up into their groups and the moment Tara had been waiting for finally came. She was about to start her first ever day of proper gymnastics training.

They all found a space on the floor and Lucy led them through a warm-up. It was very similar to the warm-up Tara had made up for herself in the garden, and she was pleased that she'd been doing everything right.

After that, they moved on to easy skills like

forward and backward rolls and headstands. Tara loved doing headstands and she held hers steadily until her face was bright red.

"Great headstand, Tara!" Lucy grinned, and if Tara wasn't already pink from being upside down, she would definitely have blushed when everyone turned to look at her.

They spent the whole morning working on floor skills. Tara loved being in the gym and working on the soft, springy floor, but she hoped they would move on to do some more difficult things later. So far, it was all a bit easy. She knew it would take much longer than a week to learn anything really amazing, but she couldn't help wishing Lucy would help them work on walkovers or handsprings.

At lunchtime, they sat on the grass outside with their packed lunches. Some of Tara's group were pairs and trios of friends, but a couple of them didn't know anyone else either. Tara took a gulp of water, then a nervous breath, and started a conversation with a girl called Amy.

"I've never done any gym, except at school," Amy admitted, when Tara asked her. "I've got to do something in the holidays while Mum's at work, and I thought this might be fun. Next week I'm going to an art club every day."

"I'd come here again next week if I could," said Tara. She couldn't imagine just doing gym for one week and replacing it with art the next. This was the most important week of the whole summer holiday.

"Have you done much gym before?" Amy asked. "You're good."

"I just practise in the garden," Tara replied. "I've never been to a gym club before."

"I wonder what we'll do after lunch," said Amy. She stretched her legs out, basking in the warm sunshine.

Hopefully something a bit more difficult, Tara thought.

✸ ✸ ✸

The afternoon *was* more difficult, and Tara soon wished it wasn't.

"Has anyone used a vault before?" Lucy asked, when they had warmed up again after the hour lunch break.

Some of the group nodded, but lots of them shook their heads and looked worried. Tara was in the second category. They'd only done floor stuff at school, and once or twice they'd practised climbing and swinging on the wall bars. She'd never even seen a vaulting table in real life – only on TV.

"Don't worry," Lucy reassured them. "We'll start with the basics, and Greg and I will help you."

They started by learning how to run along the track and jump onto the springboard so that they landed with both feet at the same time. Next, Greg asked Natasha, a fourteen year old who had been coming to the summer camp for a few years, to demonstrate a vault he called a "squat on". Natasha ran towards the vaulting table, which was square and mostly flat, but curved down a bit at the front. It was held up underneath by one thick metal leg in the middle. It seemed impossibly high, even though Lucy had set it lower than usual to make it easier.

Tara watched anxiously as Natasha jumped onto the springboard and reached her hands out towards the beige vault. Her feet bounced off the springboard and landed in between her hands on the vault, so that she was crouching on the top of it. Then she stood up and jumped neatly off, landing on the big mat on the other side. She made it look easy.

"Well done," nodded Greg. "Who's next?" Tara and Amy edged towards the back of the group. Others had a go; some of them managed it on the first try, but a few of them didn't. Soon it was Tara's turn.

She took a deep breath and tried to imagine herself as one of the Olympic gymnasts she'd seen flying over the vault on TV. She set off at a run.

The vault loomed in front of her, getting closer and closer. She jumped onto the springboard nervously, and instantly lost momentum. She teetered on the edge and almost toppled forward into the vault. She stopped herself with her hands and leaned against the curved part, defeated.

"Attack it with more confidence," advised Greg.

"You won't hurt yourself," Lucy assured her. "I'll help you."

"Whatever you do," said Greg, "don't slow down."

Tara went back to the beginning of the track to have another go. This time, she kept her speed up and when her feet hit the springboard, she didn't stop. She felt Lucy's hands on her hips, giving her a little extra push to help her up. Once she was on the vault, she was fine. It was easy enough to stand up and do a simple straight jump off. But she couldn't forget that she hadn't been able to do the whole thing by herself like Natasha. She joined the back of the line again and looked wistfully over at the floor area. Earlier, she'd felt like the summer camp was too easy. Now she was learning something new. And it was much tougher than she'd imagined.

As the week went on, Tara got to try lots of new things. She loved working on the trampoline, where Lucy taught her to do light, bouncy handsprings. And the beam was fun too, though she couldn't do anything more than walk up and down on her tiptoes, and balance with one leg held out straight behind her in an arabesque. She sort of got used to the vault, though she still felt scared every time she ran towards it, and hated feeling like she wasn't any good at it. Her favourite thing by far was the time they spent on the floor. Lucy was impressed that Tara could do the splits and could hold a bridge with her feet together and her legs straight.

On the last day of the camp, Tara was practising walkovers when she thought no one was looking.

She couldn't resist trying them on a real gym floor while she had the chance.

"Tara!" exclaimed Lucy. "You never said you could do walkovers!"

"I didn't want to show off," Tara mumbled, embarrassed because now it looked like she *was* showing off.

"Show me again," said Lucy. "I'll see if I can give you some tips." Tara showed the coach what she hoped was a good walkover. "You mustn't let your knees bend as you're going over," said Lucy. "Good try, though."

Not good enough, thought Tara. Floor skills were just about the only thing she *could* do – it would be nice to do something perfectly to make up for the disaster on the vault. She'd just have to keep practising. With that in mind, she got back to work and didn't notice Lucy go out to the lobby, or come back in with another coach. She didn't even notice when the other coach stayed to watch the last half hour of training.

At the very end, they all sat on the floor and Lucy got up to talk.

"You've all been brilliant, and I hope you've enjoyed the week," she began. "If you would like to join the club, Michelle and Greg are handing round leaflets now with the details of the group we think would be best for you."

Tara glanced around as the two coaches stepped between them all, giving them slips of paper. Amy, sitting next to Tara, was handed one about a group on Saturday afternoons. But Greg walked off without giving Tara anything. Had she been so terrible at vault that they didn't want her at all? Should she ask Lucy? Maybe it was better not to say anything – she couldn't bear to hear someone say out loud that she just wasn't good enough to be a gymnast.

She was so lost in these thoughts that she nearly jumped right off the floor when a woman spoke next to her.

"You're Tara Bailey – is that right?" she asked.

"Yes," Tara said. She turned to the woman, worried that she'd miss Lucy saying something important.

"I'm Clare Roberts. I coach one of the Acrobatic Gymnastics competition squads," the woman said with a friendly smile. "You did really well just now. Lucy told me you've been her star gymnast all week."

"Really?" Tara smiled uncertainly. She was shocked – a star gymnast? *Her?* She felt like she'd done fairly well at some things, but had she really been *good*? And then there was the vault. Surely Lucy and Clare had both made a mistake? She wasn't sure what Acrobatic Gymnastics was, or where this conversation was going.

"What gymnastics training have you done before this?" Clare asked.

"None," Tara replied. "I mean, a bit at school, and I practise a lot in the garden, but that probably doesn't count."

"None at all?" Clare sounded very surprised.

"You mean you taught yourself to do walkovers and everything else you were doing just now?"

Tara nodded and went red. In the last half hour of the day, she'd realized that she might never get another chance to work on a real floor area, so she'd practised everything she could do. She'd had no idea anyone was watching.

"Usually when people join the club we put them into Artistic Gymnastics groups – you know, working on beam, bars, vault and floor," said Clare. "But I need a new gymnast for my Acro squad. That's where gymnasts work in pairs and trios. One of my gymnasts moved into a more advanced squad, leaving one of the girls without a partner. I'd really like you to give it a try – you've obviously got the potential to be a good gymnast and you're the perfect height to work with Lindsay. What do you think?"

"Oh…um…thank you," stammered Tara.

"We train three times a week – Wednesdays, Fridays and Saturdays. You can stay for the training session tonight, if you want, to see if you like it. It starts in about twenty minutes."

Tara was too stunned to reply. She remembered the gymnasts she'd seen on the breakfast show the other day and the amazing things they could do working together.

"Will I be able to do it?" she asked nervously. "I mean…are the gymnasts in your group really good?"

"It's a competition squad, so I expect a high standard from them," said Clare. "You'll have to work hard to catch up, but from what I've seen you do today, I think you're definitely capable. It's a shame you didn't start when you were younger."

Tara nodded, even though she still felt a bit uncertain. She *had* to give it a go, didn't she? This was what she'd dreamed about. If she said no just because she was scared, she knew she'd regret it for ever. But part of her just wanted to go on as she was, by herself in the garden, with no one to laugh at her if she did things wrong. The other gymnasts in Clare's group had probably been coming here for ages. They all knew each other. And she was sure they were all going to be much, much better at gymnastics than her.

Chapter Six

Lucy called for quiet, and everyone stopped talking. "Just before you all go home, it's Tara's birthday tomorrow, so let's sing 'Happy Birthday'!"

Tara smiled at Lucy while everyone sang. Then they got to their feet and there was the bustle of leaving and saying goodbye. It took a while because everyone wanted to thank the coaches.

"Have fun on the art course!" Tara said to Amy.

"Thanks," said Amy. "I hope you have a great birthday."

Tara smiled and then Clare took her to the lobby to sort everything out with Mum. More gymnasts were arriving for their training sessions and Tara wondered which ones were in Clare's group. The coach explained Acrobatic Gymnastics to Mum and told her a bit about the group, how often they trained and how much it would cost. Tara drank some water and ate a cereal bar while she waited for Clare to finish talking.

"Is this definitely what you want to do?" Mum asked Tara.

"*Definitely!*" Tara replied. She was more sure about this than she'd ever been about anything. Clare went to the office to get some forms that Mum would have to fill in.

"It's great that Clare wants you to join her group," said Mum. "I know how hard you've been practising in the garden. But if it's too hard, or if you don't enjoy it, you don't have to carry on."

"Thanks, Mum," Tara said, giving her a hug.

When all the forms were signed, Mum said goodbye and promised to come back in two hours to pick her up. Clare and Tara went back into the gym.

The summer camp gymnasts had left, and the floor was now taken up by a group of girls and boys of mixed ages who were stretching and chatting. Clare and Tara went over to them, and the coach introduced her. Most of them smiled and said hi. Tara noticed that they were all wearing leotards in different colours and patterns, and she suddenly felt embarrassed by her T-shirt and shorts. She thought longingly of the leotard she'd seen in the shop, but then put that firmly out of her mind. She was here to learn gymnastics, she told herself – nothing else mattered.

Even though Tara was already warmed up from working hard all day, she sat down with the others and did some stretches. At the summer camp, one of the coaches had always led the warm-up, but it looked like Clare's group were left to get on with it themselves. Probably, after years of training three times a week, they knew how to do a good warm-up, Tara thought. She copied them and tried not to make it too obvious that she didn't know exactly what to do. She could hear whispers going round the group though, and she guessed they were talking about her. Her cheeks burned and she looked down so that she didn't have to see them all watching her as she moved into a straddle stretch with her legs out to the sides and her stomach on the floor. But when she sat up again, she accidentally caught the eye of a girl with long blonde hair – who gave her such a friendly smile that she suddenly felt like everything might be okay after all.

When their muscles were ready to work, the gymnasts moved into three lines at the edge of the floor. Tara wondered what was going on.

"Forward roll to straddle standing, then up to headstand," called Clare. The girls at the front of each line began to do the move across the floor.

"This bit goes on for a while," said the girl who had smiled at her. She was tall and thin and her hair swung behind her in a long ponytail. "We do loads of different moves, starting off easy and getting harder. It's sort of an extension of the warm-up. Once we've done stretches and stuff, we practise some basic moves before we start to work on new skills."

Tara nodded. They had done something similar on the summer camp. Forward rolls and headstands were fine, but how difficult would it get towards the end?

To her relief, Tara kept up well with the others to begin with. She could see them sneaking glances at her, eager to see what the new girl could do. She was pleased when Clare asked for handstand-bridge-to-stand – she bet the others would think she couldn't do it. She couldn't help smiling as she stepped up into a handstand, then brought her feet all the way over to land in a bridge position.

As soon as her feet touched the floor she pushed off with her hands and stood up. She'd done it so many times in the garden that she could perform the whole thing in one fluid movement. She did them all the way across the floor, hoping that the others were watching.

But the next one was forward walkovers. Tara watched, worried, while the first row went. They could all do it. One of the second row struggled. When the third row started, she watched the blonde girl step effortlessly into a smooth, flexible walkover. Now it was her turn. She looked at Clare.

"Don't worry if you can't do it," the coach said. "Just have a go."

Tara tried. The first and second rows had finished now, so there were six gymnasts watching her from the other side of the floor. She got as far as stepping forward onto her hands, and bringing her legs over one at a time, but she couldn't stand up. She pushed her hands off the floor and eventually managed to get back up, but it wasn't one movement like it should have been.

"Good try," Clare said, encouraging her. Tara felt better when she saw that one of the other gymnasts in her row could only do very messy walkovers too. She kept trying all the way across to the other side, but she didn't manage it properly. She hoped that backward walkovers would be next – at least she could do those.

They were next, but she realized she wasn't doing *those* right either. She watched the others first. Their legs were perfectly straight as they went over, most of them even passing through the splits. After her talk with Lucy earlier, Tara guessed hers didn't look quite so impressive.

"Try to straighten your legs, Tara," said Clare, when she did her first one. She did try, but it was much harder when you couldn't cheat by bending them. She couldn't get all the way over with straight legs. She tried all the way across until the last one, and then gave in and did it the old way.

She just wanted to feel like she could do it again, like she had the first time she'd managed it in her bedroom. But now she knew she was cheating, it didn't feel as good. She sighed and leaned against the wall, while she waited for the next instruction.

She knew her handsprings weren't very good as soon as she saw the others landing with only a little bend of the knees. Her own handsprings landed in a deep squat – almost sitting down. She did her best, and was relieved when Clare told everyone that was enough. If they'd had to practise anything more difficult, she wouldn't have been able to do it at all. She'd known that real gymnastics would be hard work, but she hadn't expected to be so far behind everyone else. When they did gymnastics at school, and when she was practising in the garden, she'd felt like she was doing well. Maybe she was a terrible gymnast after all.

"You did pretty well," Clare said to her as the group drifted, still chatting, into pairs, trios and one group of four boys, "especially as you haven't had any proper training before." Tara wondered if Clare was just trying to make her feel better. "I think it's remarkable that you managed to teach yourself all that," said Clare. Tara's face lit up. Did the coach really think that?

"Yeah," a girl with short brown hair chimed in. "I couldn't do half of that floor stuff when I first started. It took me ages and ages to do a backward walkover."

"You have got into some bad habits," Clare said to Tara, "but those can be sorted out."

Tara smiled, determined to work hard once again.

"This is Lindsay," said Clare, putting her hand on the shoulder of the blonde girl who had smiled at Tara and explained the second part of the warm-up. "I think you two will work well together. I know you've never done balances before, so we need to get started on that right away. You'll be the top, Tara, and Lindsay's the base. We can probably skip the really basic ones and start with standing on shoulders."

Tara's eyes opened wide. She wasn't sure she'd be able to do this. She looked at tall, thin Lindsay, and thought the girl couldn't possibly be strong enough to lift her all on her own.

"Don't worry." Lindsay smiled, seeing Tara's fear. "I've been a base for a few years, and you're tiny. I can easily take your weight. We can start with me kneeling down."

Clare showed Tara how to get up into the balance by standing behind Lindsay and holding her up-stretched hands. She put one foot hesitantly on Lindsay's shoulder, and looked anxiously at the coach.

"Go on," said Clare. "I'll support you." Tara gripped Lindsay's hands tightly and pulled herself up so that she was standing on the taller girl's shoulders. She could feel Clare holding her waist so she knew she wouldn't fall.

"Good," said Clare. "Now straighten your

knees. Let go of Lindsay's hands." Tara did. She was surprised – it was much easier than she'd thought. Clare's hands were only just supporting her, and soon the coach let go completely. Lindsay's hands held the backs of Tara's calves. She was balancing all by herself.

"How do I get down?" she asked.

"Take Lindsay's hands again." Tara did as she was told. "Now bring your feet down between her arms so that you land on the floor in front of her." Tara half stepped, half jumped down, and only wobbled a tiny bit when she landed on the floor, her feet neatly together and her arms in front.

"You're a natural," said Clare, grinning.

Later, Clare showed Tara how to do the balance with Lindsay standing up. To get up onto her shoulders at that height, she had to put her right foot on Lindsay's right thigh from behind, holding the taller girl's hands. She used this position as a step to put her left foot on Lindsay's left shoulder.

Lindsay straightened her legs and brought her feet together while Tara pulled her other foot up to the other shoulder. They were still holding hands, so Tara was bending forwards. She could see some of the others watching from across the floor.

"Now try to let go of Lindsay's hands and straighten up," called Clare. Tara didn't think she could. Her knees were bent and unsteady, there was only room for half of each foot on Lindsay's shoulders and she was sure she could never stand up straight. "Go on, Tara," urged Clare. "There are mats if you fall."

Tara let go. Lindsay moved her hands to hold the backs of Tara's legs…but Tara was still leaning forward too much. She tried desperately to grip Lindsay's shoulders with her toes but it was no good. She tumbled forwards onto the mat at Clare's feet.

"Sorry," she said to the coach, rubbing her elbow where she'd knocked it on the floor. She tried not to cry. She wanted to be a good gymnast so much and she wanted to show the others that she could be part of this group. Now she was messing everything up.

"Don't worry. It's difficult when you're first learning. You'll get there." Clare was surprisingly comforting. "Ready to go up again?"

Tara got to her feet and nodded, determined. Now that she'd fallen once, she knew that it didn't really hurt, so she wasn't scared of that any more. But she was afraid that she'd *never* be able to do the balance. She was afraid that she would fail on her first day in Clare's group, and that would be the end of her gymnastics dream.

She tried again, and fell again. Her eyes filled with tears, but she refused to let them spill onto her cheeks. Up on Lindsay's shoulders a third time, she managed to stand up and stretch her arms to the ceiling.

"Good!" said Clare. "Now straighten those knees!" Tara did, and found that it was easier to hold the balance when all her muscles were working hard. She felt like she was on top of the entire universe! "Okay, take Lindsay's hands to come down," Clare told her. Lindsay let go of her legs and Tara looked down to find her hands. But before she could hold onto them, she was falling forwards again. She was frustrated, but Clare was pleased that she'd managed the balance.

Again and again they tried, and by the time they finished, Tara had performed three successful balances. She was exhausted, but she felt great.

Everyone stopped to have a drink of water and Clare went to talk to another coach by the door to the lobby. Tara remembered that she'd left her water bottle in the lobby and ran off to get it. She grabbed the bottle from her bag and gulped water down for a few seconds, before wandering back towards the gym, glancing at the photos on the walls again as she passed them. Then she noticed that another gymnast from her group was standing in the lobby. She was tall and strong, and looked a bit older than most of the others. She had dyed blonde hair and blue eyes that Tara remembered staring at her when she was learning to stand on Lindsay's shoulders. The girl was standing by the door into the gym, and as Tara got closer, she heard voices coming from just beyond the door, and realized that the older gymnast was listening to Clare's conversation. Tara paused, not knowing what to do. The other girl hadn't noticed her.

"...it's only her first session, of course. It's too early to tell," Clare was saying. Tara's heart started beating faster. They were talking about her.

"From what you've said it sounds like you're right," said the other coach. Right about what? Tara wished she'd reached the lobby a few seconds earlier.

"We'll see," replied Clare. "She'll be one to keep an eye on, anyway..."

The voices moved away, and the older gymnast went back into the gym. Tara wondered if the girl heard the whole conversation. *One to keep an eye on.* What did that mean? Did Clare think she was doing well in her first session? Or did they have to keep an eye on her because she wasn't going to cope with the difficult skills she was trying to learn?

There was one gymnast who knew what Clare had said, and that thought made Tara feel uncomfortable.

Next, Tara's group worked on the trampoline. Some of the gymnasts practised somersaults – one or two were beginning to learn to do them with twists. Clare told Tara to stick to handsprings for today. When Lucy had worked with her on them during the summer camp, Tara had been thrilled to find that handsprings were much easier on the bouncy trampoline than they were in the garden. *If only the floor was as bouncy*, she thought. They had to take turns on the trampoline, so while they waited, the gymnasts chatted together. They were all eager to talk to Tara. A small dark-haired girl with olive skin and large brown eyes came and sat next to her on the edge of the tumbling track.

"Hey, it's Tara, right?" She smiled. "I'm Jasmine. That's Sophie." Jasmine pointed out a taller girl who was doing a handstand behind them. "We'll be in Year Ten at school together in September, although I'm so short you'd never know I was fourteen!" Jasmine laughed and Tara immediately felt at ease with her.

"I'm Megan." The girl with short brown hair who'd spoken to Tara earlier jumped into the conversation. "I'm Sophie's partner. You already know Lindsay – she's thirteen. And so am I," she gabbled, clearly not willing to let anyone do their own introductions. Tara looked over at Lindsay, who was bouncing high into the air on the trampoline. She couldn't believe her new partner was only two years older than her – Lindsay was seriously tall for her age. "This is Sam, Jasmine's partner," Megan continued as the girl Tara had seen in the lobby came over to them. "She's the oldest in the group. The bossiest, too."

"How old are you, anyway?" demanded Sam, ignoring Megan. She crossed her arms and stared at Tara.

"I'll be eleven tomorrow," Tara answered.

"And you've never done gym before?" she sneered. "I just hope you're up to it, that's all. I don't know why Clare put you in a competition squad. Silverdale's got a great reputation for Acro. We don't need anyone messing up our chances next time we compete. Clare should have got someone who's actually *done* gymnastics before."

Tara felt her face going bright red and she didn't know where to look. Did everyone else think the same thing as Sam? Maybe it was to do with what Clare had said to the other coach. Whatever it was, Sam had overhead it. Was that why she was being so nasty?

"Ignore her," murmured Megan, as Sam turned away to watch Lindsay practising front somersaults on the trampoline. "She's just jealous that *she* wasn't in this group at your age. Honestly, she's only fifteen, but she acts like she's *twenty* the way she talks to us!"

Sam turned back to the group and raised an eyebrow at Tara. "As long as you know it's not going to be all glitter and glory and medals. We work *hard* at this club. Probably harder than you've ever worked in your life." She walked away to talk to two of the boys.

"She's okay once you get to know her," said Jasmine. "I've been her Acro partner for three years, and she can be nice sometimes."

"You'd just better hope *you're* not ever partnered with her," Megan whispered to Tara. "I was, when I first started. Tough work, I can tell you. If anything went wrong it was always my fault – she'd never admit when she made a mistake!"

Tara's turn on the trampoline was next, so Megan didn't have time to tell her who the four boys and three other girls in the group were. Tara already had a lot to think about as she began bouncing though. She could feel Sam's eyes on her, noticing every little mistake she made, but she tried hard to ignore it and think only about how to do a perfect handspring. When she bounced off onto the crash mat, she found Clare at her side.

"You've done really well today, Tara," said the coach.

"Not well enough," mumbled Tara. "There's loads I can't do."

"You've certainly got passion," said Clare. "And that's key for a good gymnast. I think you've got natural talent as well." She nodded towards the trampoline. "You seemed very confident up there."

"I just sort of forgot about everything else," said Tara.

"I think you're going to do very well here," said Clare. "If you want to come back, that is?"

"Definitely!" Tara grinned. "I love it already."

"Good," laughed Clare. "How about you start properly on Wednesday? Your mum said it's your birthday tomorrow, so I'm sure you'd like to spend the day with your friends." She looked at the clock above the double doors. "Time's up!" she called towards the group. "See you on Wednesday," she said to Tara with a smile.

Tara smiled back. "I can't wait." And it was true – she couldn't wait for more gymnastics. But she wasn't looking forward to seeing Sam again.

Chapter Seven

The next day was Tara's eleventh birthday. She woke up early with the sun in her eyes, and snuggled further under the bedcovers, grinning to herself and thinking about the party she was having later that day. Emily and Kate were coming, of course, and some other friends from school. They were going to have a barbecue in the garden and then her two best friends were sleeping over.

She could hear the sounds of Mum and Dad getting up and going downstairs, so she scrambled out of bed and hurried down to see them.

"Happy birthday!" they said and both hugged her at the same time. There was a stack of presents wrapped in pink paper on the kitchen table, and Mum had already set four places. Birthdays always meant special breakfasts in the Bailey house. Tara stared at the presents and the pile of cards in front of her plate.

"Not until Anna's up," said Dad, who could tell she was itching to open them.

Tara grinned, headed for the door and dashed up the stairs and into Anna's bedroom.

"Wake up!" she shouted, laughing. Anna was curled up in her bed, talking to her favourite toy cat.

"Kitty says happy birthday," said Anna.

"Don't you want breakfast, Anna? Mum's making pancakes."

Anna was out of bed instantly, Kitty forgotten

on her pillow. The sisters raced each other down the stairs to sit at the table. Mum made the pancakes while Tara opened her birthday cards – from aunts and uncles and cousins, from Mum and Dad, and one that Anna had made herself. She'd folded a piece of white card and tried to draw a gymnast on the front. Inside, she'd written (probably with help from Mum):

To Tara,
happy birthday
I love you lots
from Anna xxxxx

Tara smiled at the six-year-old scrawl and stood the card up next to her glass of juice. Presents were next – some of her relatives had sent money in their cards, but there was a parcel from Auntie Hazel. She opened the pretty pink and silver paper to find three new books. She skimmed over the backs to see what they were about – they all sounded great.

"Let's see," said Mum, turning around from the cooker. Tara handed her the books and picked up the present from Anna. It was obvious that Mum had wrapped it up. Tara guessed that she'd chosen it, too – it was a lovely new top that Tara had seen a few weeks ago in one of the shops in town. It was pale blue with little white flowers scattered over it. Tara decided she'd wear it for the party later.

"Thanks, Anna!" she said.

There were three presents from Mum and Dad – a film on DVD that she'd asked for and a new pair of jeans were the first two. When she came to the third one, Mum and Dad looked at each other and smiled. Tara unfolded the paper carefully and gasped when she saw what was inside. It was the beautiful black and silver leotard! She held it up to look at it properly. The silver sparkles glittered like tiny stars and the velvety material felt soft in her hands. There was also a black velvet scrunchie to go with it.

"Thank you," she gushed, leaping up to hug Mum and then Dad. She couldn't wait to try it on – but she'd have to, as just then Mum put the plate of pancakes down in the middle of the table. Dad cleared away the wrapping paper and sat down, then he held up his glass of juice in a toast.

"Happy birthday, Tara," he said. "Eleven years old!"

"Happy birthday!" echoed Mum and Anna, and everyone clinked their glasses together.

As soon as breakfast was finished, Tara ran up to her room to try on her new leotard. The moment she'd pulled it on, she stood in front of the mirror and scraped her hair back into a ponytail with the matching scrunchie. Then she stretched her arms up as if she was just about to begin a routine, watching the silver sparkles shine in her reflection. A shiver of excitement ran through her – the girl in the mirror was really a gymnast! She just wished she didn't have to wait until Wednesday to wear the leotard at Silverdale – that felt like ages away.

Tara was restless all morning. She started reading one of her new books, but she kept thinking about the party later. She tried watching TV with Anna, but she couldn't focus on that either. Then she thought about working on her solo routine for the dance show with Kate and Emily, but even that couldn't stop her imagining how much fun the party was going to be!

Finally, Mum gave her some balloons to blow up, and she began to feel like the party was actually getting closer. Outside, she and Anna tied streamers and balloons to branches and chairs and the washing line – anything they could reach. Tara had to move most of Anna's, because she tied them onto branches that were too low down.

Mum banned Tara from the kitchen, where the birthday cake was being iced. So instead she went to help Dad set the barbecue up, but she made sure not to get any dust from the coals on her new clothes.

At last evening came. Emily was the first to arrive for the party. Her brother Adam, who was in Anna's class at school, came too. Kate was next, and Tara rushed them both up to her room to show them the new leotard.

"It's pretty," said Emily.

"Yeah," agreed Kate. "Really nice." But they were more interested in the new top and jeans she was wearing.

Other girls and boys from school began to arrive then, so they went back downstairs. Dad got the barbecue started and set up his laptop and some speakers so that they could have music in the garden. Soon everyone was chatting and singing along.

Some of the boys found a football and began to kick it about with Adam and Anna, while Tara and the girls sat in a circle on the grass, talking and giggling. Then the football got stuck in the hedge, so the boys started to play chase instead. Matt, who was usually quiet at school, tore across the garden trying to catch someone, but tripped and fell into Emily on the ground.

"Sorry!" he said quickly. When he saw Emily wasn't hurt, he grinned cheekily, then tapped her arm. "You're it!" he said, and leaped up to run away. Emily sprang to her feet and chased after him. The other girls, laughing, got up to join in the game.

Finally worn out, they all sat on the ground eating burgers and hot dogs, and then bowls of ice cream, which Tara and her friends covered in chocolate sauce and brightly coloured sweets. When it began to get dark, Mum brought the birthday cake out. It was covered in pink icing and in the middle was a small figure of a gymnast in the splits, made from fondant icing. *It must have taken Mum ages*, Tara thought. The light from the candles glowed on the faces of all Tara's friends, and she put her arms around Kate and Emily while everyone sang "Happy Birthday". She blew the candles out in one go, and made a secret wish – but anyone who knew her could guess what it was: to be an amazing gymnast.

Her friends' parents started to arrive after that, and soon it was just Kate and Emily left. Mum and Dad helped them to put mattresses, pillows and sleeping bags down on the living room floor and then gave them a useless warning about noise before going upstairs.

The girls watched a film and started a game of Cluedo, but mostly they just talked. It took a long time for them to get worn out, for their giggles to stop and their heads to fall onto pillows. Tara didn't want to sleep, and she wasn't tired. It had been the most brilliant week of her life, and this was the perfect way to end it.

"Em," she whispered. "Are you awake?"

Emily turned over to face her. "Yeah," she whispered back. "Kate?"

"I'm awake too," came a murmur from the

other side of the room. Kate got up and tiptoed across to the sofa where Tara lay.

Tara sat up on the sofa to make room for Kate. Emily curled up and hugged her knees on the mattress next to it.

"Come up here," offered Tara. She and Kate were sitting under Tara's duvet, and they moved along to make room for Emily.

"You never finished telling us about your gymnastics club," said Emily. Tara had started to tell them earlier about joining Clare's group, but then everyone else had arrived and there hadn't been time to explain everything. "I can't believe you're a real gymnast at *Silverdale* now!" said Emily. "Will you learn to do all the difficult things they do in the display?"

"Was it amazing?" asked Kate.

"*So* amazing," Tara sighed. She told them everything – all about the gym and Clare and Lindsay and Sam; about how much fun it had been to work on a real floor area, and her worries about being behind the others. She hadn't even told Mum that. Somehow, it was easier to talk about it in the middle of the night – secrets and worries were what sleepovers were for.

"Maybe you should just try to focus on the exciting parts and not worry so much about trying to catch up?" suggested Kate.

"Yeah," agreed Emily. "It must feel horrible to be so worried about that, and you do gym because you enjoy it, right?"

"Like our dance show," added Kate. "We're only doing it because it's fun. It doesn't matter if we're not completely perfect."

Tara knew they were only trying to help, but they didn't really understand what it was like to love gymnastics so much, and want to be the best she could possibly be, yet feel so far behind everyone else. It *wasn't* like the dance show to her – gymnastics mattered so much more.

She hoped that after training for a while she would start to catch up to the others. But what if she never did? No matter how many times she reminded herself that Clare had chosen *her*, she couldn't shake the feeling that maybe Sam was right – maybe Clare should have picked someone who'd been training for years.

Chapter Eight

Wednesday couldn't come soon enough. Tara had managed to push her worries aside for the moment and was desperate to get back to the gym and wear her new leotard for the first time. Her group's training session started at five in the evening. Clare's competition group trained all year round and even though it was the summer holidays, their training sessions were in the evenings because that's when they would continue once everyone went back to school. Tara counted the hours and minutes all day. She was ready to go ages before she needed to be and then she bugged Mum so much about being on time that they arrived at the gym early.

"Bye!" Tara yelled, slamming the car door shut and heading for the main entrance.

Mum laughed. "Anyone would think you'd been away from the gym for weeks, not days!" she called through the open window.

The changing room was almost empty. Tara put her bag down on a bench and changed into the beautiful black leotard. She went over to the mirror and checked her hair, which she'd already tied back in a ponytail.

While she was doing this, Jasmine came in. Tara smiled, glad to see someone she knew. Jasmine said hi to a few of the girls who were getting changed or sitting chatting. Then she came over to talk to Tara.

"Hi, Tara! I'm glad you came back," she said.

"Of course I did!" laughed Tara.

"You never know," Jasmine replied. "Clare works us pretty hard."

"I want to work hard," Tara said.

Jasmine grinned. "Then you'll fit right in."

"Ooh, Tara, I love your leotard!" gushed Megan, coming into the changing room with Sophie.

The sound of voices rose as the room filled up. It was nearly five o'clock. Sophie started a conversation with Jasmine about something she'd been working on the week before, Megan chattered away to anyone who was listening and Tara could hear at least three other conversations going on as well – people talking about TV shows and music and gymnastics all at the same time. Then she heard a quiet voice beside her ear.

"I think Clare wants to get us going on some other balances today." It was Lindsay, in a lovely dark green leotard with a strip of white that twisted like a ribbon in a similar pattern to the silver sparkles on Tara's new leotard.

"Cool." Tara nodded. "Is it time to go in yet?"

"Yeah, come on. It's too noisy in here."

Clare was waiting for them in the gym. Sam was there too, with a couple of the boys. Tara caught the older girl rolling her eyes at them when she and Lindsay walked in.

After the warm-up, stretching, and performing moves across the floor, the gymnasts sorted themselves out into their usual pairs and groups. The four boys worked together – three were tall and looked strong, and the fourth one was tiny. He looked about Tara's age, and she could see why he needed to be small; the other boys lifted him high into the air and threw him into somersaults as if he weighed nothing. Tara was starting to realize that, in gymnastics, being short for your age wasn't a bad thing at all.

Clare worked with Tara and Lindsay again for most of the session. The others knew what they were doing and what they needed to practise, but Tara was learning everything from the beginning.

She was amazed by all the different balances she and Lindsay could do. Even though she was just starting to learn Acrobatic Gymnastics skills, there were lots of basic balances that she knew she'd be able to manage with a bit of work. Her favourite was one where Lindsay kneeled with one knee on the floor and one foot planted securely in front of her to keep her steady. Her thigh was horizontal, almost like part of a beam. Tara stood to one side of her and put her hands on her thigh, while Lindsay held her waist, one arm going across Tara's front to hold the other side. Then, with a push off the floor and lift from Lindsay's hands, Tara was upside down with her knees tucked in to her chest. After a bit more practice, she could straighten her legs up into a handstand. She came down grinning, and then caught Jasmine and Sam watching them. Jasmine gave her a big smile, but Sam shrugged and muttered something about the balance being easy.

"Don't go just yet!" called Clare, when the

session finished. Megan, who had made it halfway to the door already, bounded back to the rest of the group. "Make sure you're all here on Friday – we're going to be working on the routine for the Summer Display."

Tara wondered if that included her.

"Tara," said Clare, as if she could read her mind, "we've been working on the display for the last month or so, but if you can learn the routine quickly you can be in it." Tara was thrilled. She'd only been a Silverdale gymnast for a few days and already she was going to be in a display! She wondered what kind of routine it would be – balances, probably. Maybe she would get to include some of her new skills with Lindsay.

She told Mum about it on the way home, and then phoned Emily as soon as she got through the front door.

"Hi, Tara," Emily answered.

"I'm going to be in a gym display!" Tara squeaked.

Emily laughed at her excitement. "The Silverdale Summer Display?" she asked. "The one we've been going to watch for years at the summer fête?"

"Yes!" Tara replied, still giddy from the thrill of her news.

"That's amazing!" said Emily, almost as enthusiastic as Tara. "Tell me everything." But just then, Mum called Tara to have dinner.

"Gotta go," said Tara. "But we're going to Kate's tomorrow afternoon, aren't we? To practise for our dance show. I promise I won't stop talking about it then."

"I believe that," Emily laughed. "See you tomorrow."

Tara was glad she was going to see her friends the next day. She couldn't wait to tell them all about her experiences at Silverdale. After all, she wasn't going back to the club for two whole days, and she knew it was going to feel like for ever.

Chapter Nine

Clare's group were going to perform all together for the display. The coach had chosen a summery pop song, and worked out a routine, which she'd already taught to the rest of the group. Tara had to learn fast. For the next two weeks, they hardly worked on anything else.

The routine had some quick dance sections that Tara found tricky to learn at first, and she just knew that Sam was watching every mistake she made.

Summertime and Somersaults

Lindsay turned out to be a great dancer though, and she helped Tara go through the difficult bits slowly until she'd got them. As well as the dance moves, the gymnasts were going to perform balances in their usual pairs, trio and the boys' four. With all of them doing different balances at the same time, the routine was busy and exciting.

Everyone's favourite part was when they all came down from different balances in their pairs and groups and went straight into handsprings. Tara knew it would look fantastic when they'd got the timing perfect, but there was a problem: she couldn't do it. Working on the trampoline and tumbling track had helped with her handsprings, but on the floor they were still not as good as the others'. None of them said anything, but she saw the looks Sam kept giving the boys.

When she wasn't at the gym, Tara spent a lot of time at home practising the routine in the garden. She hadn't forgotten the dance show with Kate and Emily, either, and she found time to work out a gymnastics routine for that too. When she added in afternoons at the shopping centre with her friends, and rainy days practising their dances in Kate's living room, she was so busy that she hardly had time to think. Kate had made up another dance to a beautiful, slow song and taught it to Emily and Tara. They hadn't had much time to learn it though, and Tara kept forgetting it. She'd just have to follow Kate and hope it wasn't too obvious.

All the hard work at Silverdale meant that her backward walkovers were almost perfect now. By the day of the dance show with her friends, she could just about manage a forward one too, so she decided to take a risk and add that to her solo routine. At least, performing in Kate's back garden, no one would be judging her or thinking she wasn't good enough.

It was Sunday, and Tara and Emily spent the whole day at Kate's house. They had practised the group dances in their matching outfits and they all thought they looked great. For her solo, Kate had a red and white skirt that was great for twirling, and a white top with silver sparkles. Emily was going to wear jeans and a top made of layers of floaty, lilac-coloured material. Tara, of course, had her leotard.

They rehearsed all day, and then set up the garden for the performance. They lined up chairs at one end of the grass. Emily was really good at art, and she'd made an invitation for each parent (delivered the week before when they'd spent the morning at Tara's house, the afternoon at Kate's and the evening at Emily's). When Tara's and Emily's parents arrived, Kate showed them to their seats along with her own parents. Anna sat on the ground in front of the chairs with Emily's brothers, six-year-old Adam and two-year-old Luke.

Kate fiddled with her iPod for a few seconds. The dads were all still chatting about the Grand Prix race they were missing.

"We're starting!" called Tara. She looked pleadingly at Mum, who nudged Dad and got them to stop talking. The girls ran into their starting positions, standing in a line with their backs to the audience and their heads down. The music began and they went into the first dance they'd made up, the one that had started the whole idea. It went better than it had ever done before – even Emily remembered all the steps – and the audience burst into loud applause at the end. The girls grinned at each other and at their parents.

Kate, after a lightning-quick costume change, started off the solos, because Tara and Emily had said they didn't want to go first. They got changed quickly too, and then stood to one side to watch their friend dance. Tara was impressed – Kate was great at doing all the pop star dance moves and her routine fitted really well with the song she'd chosen. Emily was next. Her dance was a strange mix of steps Kate had made up for her and sections that Emily had worked out by herself.

Tara preferred the bits Emily had done – they suited her much more.

When it was Tara's turn, she walked into the middle of the garden. In her leotard, she really felt like she could be walking out onto the floor at the Olympics. She took up her starting position, kneeling on one leg with the other pointed out to the side, and Kate started the music.

Tara had practised the routine so many times that her body naturally flowed through it. The backward walkovers, in a long diagonal line from one corner to the other, were a big success, and the forward walkover was her best yet. She jumped and turned, head held high like Beth Tweddle, and she was sad when she knew she was nearly at the end. She felt like she could keep going all afternoon and into the night. She took a deep breath, stretched her foot out in front of her and launched herself into a short run-up and a handspring. Even without the sprung floor of the gym, her landing was better than it used to be.

She stretched, performed a neat backward roll to handstand, and danced forward into her finishing position as the music ended.

"Wow!" said Dad, clapping so hard she thought his hands must hurt. Everyone else clapped too, including Kate and Emily. Tara was out of breath and full of delight. Impressing the parents was just a bonus; the best thing had been actually performing the routine. Nothing had ever felt so wonderful.

They still had one more group dance to perform, but Tara had to change back into her skirt and pink top. She ran into the house to change in the bathroom, where she'd left her clothes ready. While they waited, Kate and Emily handed round lemonade, orange juice and biscuits to the audience.

They hadn't spent as much time on the second dance, so there were moments when only Kate really knew what they were meant to be doing. They got through it and kept smiling, but Emily turned the wrong way three times and Tara lost the timing on one difficult sequence. The audience clapped at the end anyway, all except Luke, who was crawling under his dad's chair, and Adam, who was too busy pulling Anna's hair. Then the three performers came to the front and took bows while their parents cheered and clapped some more.

"Your gymnastics was great, Tara," said Mrs. Walter, Emily's mum.

"All that thumping around was worth it," joked Dad.

"Oh, stop," said Mum. "Tara, you were wonderful. So were you two," she said, turning to Kate and Emily. "I have no idea how you all remembered everything."

"I didn't," said Emily, blushing a bit.

"Didn't matter," said Kate, putting her arm around Emily. "Your routine was definitely the best though, Tara."

Tara smiled at Kate. She knew that Kate had

worked really hard on her own dance. "I could never have danced like you, though," she said.

"You were all good," said Mr. Wakefield, Kate's dad. And everyone nodded.

Later on, Emily and Kate's parents kept asking Tara about Silverdale. They sounded really impressed when she told them about doing all the different balances and that she was going to be in the Summer Display – but somehow, the conversation made Tara feel uneasy. She knew she'd done this routine well, but it was a routine full of easy stuff. And while she'd loved every second of performing, at the back of her mind was one constant thought: she wasn't any good compared to the brilliant gymnasts at Silverdale. That was the standard she'd have to live up to next time, and she just wasn't sure that she could. She was good enough for the garden, but was she ready to perform in front of half the town at the Silverdale Summer Display? She didn't think so. Not yet. And time was running out.

Chapter Ten

The dance show had been a triumph, but back at Silverdale it was hard work as usual. Other groups were using the two floor areas at the beginning of the Wednesday session, so Clare gave her gymnasts a break from rehearsing for the display. Instead, they worked on somersaults, practising on the trampoline so that they could get extra height until they were ready to try them on the tumbling track. Tara couldn't believe what she was hearing when Clare said she was going to teach her to do a front somersault. It wasn't something she had to learn for the display, but it was a skill she needed to start learning if she was going to improve her gymnastics.

"Keep your eyes up," said Clare. "If you look down you won't get enough height and then you won't have time to get your feet round."

"Okay." Tara nodded, and took a deep breath. She bounced a little on the trampoline while she found a spot to focus on, high up on the opposite wall. Then she bounced properly, once, twice, three times and then…up she went, tucking her knees in to her chest and pulling her arms in to get her body round in a front somersault…almost. She didn't get round far enough for her feet to come down, and she landed in a sitting position on the trampoline.

"Height, Tara," Clare said again. "You're still looking down, and your body goes where your eyes are looking. Don't be scared."

Summertime and Somersaults

That was easy for Clare to say, Tara thought. She wasn't the one throwing herself into the air, unable to see where she should be landing.

"Try again," the coach encouraged. In the background, Sam sighed loudly. Her turn on the trampoline was next and she was obviously getting impatient.

Look up, look up, look up, Tara repeated to herself silently. She bounced and flew up into the somersault, only tearing her eyes away from the wall at the last second, tucking her head in as her body rotated. She got her feet down on the trampoline first, but she'd rotated too far instead of not enough, and she went flying forwards onto her hands.

"Better," said Clare. Then she grinned. "Not so much rotation next time."

Tara laughed and nodded. She picked herself up and bounced off the trampoline into the foam pit next to it.

"Finally," muttered Sam, taking Tara's place

on the trampoline. Tara sat with Lindsay and Megan and watched Sam learning to do a full-twisting back somersault. Tara couldn't wait until she got onto twists. She almost laughed out loud at herself – she really was dreaming far ahead! She couldn't even do a single front somersault yet. But she knew that she would – and that brought the dream a little bit closer.

Later, she was brought back to reality by her problems with handsprings. She was so nearly able to do them properly, but Sam made it clear that nearly wasn't good enough.

"Clare, I think Tara needs some help with her handsprings," she said loudly, while they were going through the routine without the music. Everyone stopped. Most of them looked at Tara, who had gone bright red. She bit her lip; she was *not* going to cry in front of everyone. Especially not in front of Sam.

"Sam, you just focus on yourself and Jasmine and let me worry about what everyone else is doing," said Clare. "Practise your balances, please," she said to the group. "Tara, let's go up to the tumbling track. Lindsay, Jack, Mel, your handsprings could do with a bit of work too."

Tara could have hugged her coach for that – for including the others in the extra training and not singling her out.

"Sam's an idiot," Lindsay muttered as they followed Clare to the track.

"She's right though," Tara whispered. "My handsprings are rubbish."

"You're getting much better," said Mel. "I've been in this group for two years and Clare still thinks my handsprings need work! Yours'll be perfect in no time."

Tara felt a bit better, knowing that not everyone agreed with Sam. The extra help from Clare turned out to be really useful, and even though it had felt horrible, she was glad that Sam's comment had given her the chance to improve. She just hoped she'd be able to improve fast enough – the display was in three days' time.

That evening, Tara and Kate went to Emily's house. The Walters owned a bakery, and they lived in the rooms above it. They always had a stall at the town summer fête, which Emily, Tara and Kate sometimes helped with.

"Are you excited about your gym display this weekend?" asked Emily.

"I can't wait to see you perform!" said Kate.

"Oh…you don't have to come," said Tara.

"Don't be ridiculous! Of course we're coming!" said Kate.

"I really don't mind if you don't want to," said Tara. "Or if you have to help out on the bakery stall."

"Don't you want us to come?" Emily asked quietly.

"No, I do…but…" Tara trailed off.

"But what?" asked Kate. "We want to see you doing your amazing balances!"

"But I'm not amazing," Tara replied. "I'm not even *good*."

"That's not true," Kate insisted. "We've seen you doing gym in the garden, remember. We *know* you're good."

"Not compared to everyone at Silverdale!" said Tara. The tears that she'd managed to stop earlier came then, and her voice wobbled. "There's this one bit that I can't do very well, and the whole routine will get ruined, and everyone will see that I'm not good enough to be in that group."

"Oh, Tara…" said Emily, and gave her a big hug.

"You're worrying too much," said Kate. "Remember how much fun it was when we did our dances for our parents? You loved that! And your solo was brilliant."

Tara nodded tearfully. "But this is different," she said.

"Not that different," said Kate. "Your parents

are going to be there, aren't they? And the other gymnasts' parents? So it's just the same, only a bit bigger."

"That's true," sniffed Tara.

"Anyway, you *are* good enough," insisted Emily. "Your coach wouldn't have picked you for her group otherwise."

"Thanks, guys," said Tara, hugging them both again. "I'd really like you to come and watch."

"We wouldn't miss it," Emily said with a smile. She handed Tara a tissue to dry her eyes.

"Come on, let's kick the boys out of the living room," said Kate. "I want to watch a film."

Luke and Adam were about to go to bed anyway, so they had the TV to themselves. They watched *High School Musical*. Tara guessed Emily had chosen it to remind her of how much fun it was to perform. It didn't really work. It *was* fun performing something you believed you were good at, but Tara couldn't stop thinking about the one moment she was dreading: performing a handspring in front of a gym full of people and all the Silverdale coaches. And everyone would see that she wasn't as good as the others.

Chapter Eleven

The day of the town summer fête was beautiful, sunny and warm. To Tara, that meant only one thing: a lot of people were going to turn up, so the Silverdale Summer Display would have a big audience. She couldn't decide if that was a good thing or a bad thing. She had to admit she was excited to show everyone what she could do. But if she messed up, the whole town would be there to see it. Either way, the good weather made the rest of the fête more fun. Last year, it had rained and the whole thing had been miserable.

"Where shall we go next?" asked Emily as they came out of the library, which had been taken over by face-painters. They'd waited for half an hour while Adam and Anna were transformed (from the neck up) into Spider-Man and a glittery butterfly.

"Anywhere that's outside," said Kate, tipping her head back and smiling up at the clear blue sky. "It was way too stuffy in there."

"Well, that narrows the choice down to just about everything," said Tara. They were standing in the central square, which usually had a noisy market on weekends and pretty stalls that smelled like cinnamon at Christmas time. Today it was lined with stands selling cakes, toys, jewellery and plants, and quite a few with games and raffles. Tara looked at her watch. "I've got to go and get ready for the display in fifteen minutes," she said. The gymnasts had gone to the gym in the morning for a final rehearsal, then they'd been given a few hours off to have lunch and wander round the fête. They had to be back at the gym at 2.30 so that they had enough time to get changed and warm up before the display started at 3 p.m.

"Hook a Duck, maybe?" suggested Emily, thinking of Anna and her own younger brother, who was spinning round and round in dizzy circles. She was in charge of Adam for the day while her parents ran the bakery stall. Not wanting to be left out, Anna had demanded to be part of the group too.

"Yeah!" cried Anna, jumping around and clapping her hands at Emily's suggestion.

"Let's go," said Tara. "I think it's on the way to the gym, anyway."

It was funny seeing a paddling pool full of yellow plastic ducks on the pavement in the middle of town. Tara held the wooden pole she was given nervously, hoping no one from Silverdale walked past – Sam thought she was childish enough already. At the thought of Sam and the gym, her stomach tensed and she was suddenly very aware of how soon the display was. Her hands shook as she reached out with the pole, trying to push the metal hook through the ring on top of a duck's head.

"Come on, Tara," Anna said loudly. "It's easy!" She'd already caught a duck and been rewarded with a bottle of strawberry bubble bath. Kate's duck had won her some bracelets made from brightly coloured plastic beads. Lucky Emily won a small teddy bear, which Anna eyed enviously. Adam was swishing his pole through the water, making waves for the ducks to bob up and down on. At last he hooked one, and the lady running the stall turned it over to check the number written in black pen. She handed him a packet of fizzy sherbert sweets.

"Oh great," groaned Kate. "Now he'll be even more hyper."

Emily laughed. "I'll take him back to Mum and

Dad when it's time for Tara's display." Tara had just got hold of a duck, but her hand trembled at the mention of the display and the duck slipped off the hook and bobbed away. She finally caught another one and ended up with a packet of sweets like Adam's.

"Here," she said, offering them to her sister. "I'd better go to the gym."

"We'll be there early so we can get good seats," said Kate. "As soon as we've taken Anna and Adam back to the parents."

"Good luck!" said Emily, grinning. Tara felt sick.

She hurried off to the gym. Silverdale was in the centre of town, perfect for the summer fête. Tara was glad they didn't have to perform on mats in the central square like dance groups sometimes did. There was something comforting about being in the familiar gym. As soon as she stepped into the changing room, she felt a little better.

Jasmine and Sophie were sitting on a bench, already in their leotards. They were doing their hair and chatting as if it was just a normal training session. Tara smiled at them and got changed, keeping that thought in her mind.

The music for their routine was a fun pop song about summer, so they were all wearing brightly coloured leotards. Tara had been worried when Clare suggested this, as her only leotard was the black and silver one she'd got for her birthday. But Jasmine had come to the rescue and lent Tara one that was bright blue with swirls of lime green across the top. Even though Jasmine was three years older, she was very small for her age and the leotard fitted Tara well. As a bonus, it nearly matched the one Lindsay was going to wear, which was apple green.

As the changing room got busier and busier, and noisier and noisier, it became clear that this was not just any Saturday at Silverdale, however much Tara might have wished it was. The display was important for the club because it helped them to get funding and it was a good way of encouraging new people to join, so the gymnasts all had to be at their best. Tara thought about all the photos on the walls of the lobby. Clare had said that they would have a photo taken at the end of the routine, in their finishing poses. Tara was looking forward to being in a picture on one of those walls. But she had to get to the end of the routine first.

Megan was moving round their group with a can of hairspray that had glitter in it and made their hair sparkle while holding it in place.

"Close your eyes," she told Tara, and then sprayed a cloud of silvery glitter over her head. Tara turned to look in the mirror, half-expecting her whole head to be silver. It wasn't – she was still blonde but her hair, tied back in a ponytail, had a definite sparkle now. She grinned at her reflection and hoped her gymnastics would sparkle just as much.

Chapter Twelve

Out in the lobby, Tara twisted her hands together nervously and hopped about from one foot to the other.

"Stop it!" laughed Jasmine. "You'll make *me* nervous!"

Jasmine didn't have anything to be worried about, Tara thought. She was one of the best gymnasts in the group. Looking at the photos on the walls again, she recognized Jasmine and Sam in quite a few of them. In each one, they had gold medals hanging round their necks.

The afternoon was getting hotter, and the big double doors into the gym were propped open to let in air. They could hear music, and if they stood to one side of the lobby they had a clear view of the floor area. At the moment, a group of four- and five-year-old girls in pink leotards were performing a simple routine.

"Aren't they cute!" gushed Megan.

"Remember when our routines were like that?" Sophie said to Jasmine, who laughed. Tara felt another wave of worry, remembering that the others had all been doing this for a really long time. It was fine for the little girls in pink to get things wrong; they were only tiny. She was performing with gymnasts who won competitions and she just *had* to do everything perfectly.

"You'll be great," whispered Lindsay from behind her. At that moment, the little girls finished their routine and ran off the floor to their coach.

Summertime and Somersaults

Clare's group were next.

They walked out onto the floor in single file. Tara was near the end of the line, and watching the others in front of her, she suddenly felt really proud to be part of the group. Exhilaration bubbled up inside her. The colours of their leotards filled the floor as they walked to their starting positions. She knew the routine was going to be as bright and exciting as their leotards.

Just before the music started, she caught sight of Mum, Dad and Anna in the audience. Next to them were Emily and Kate. They'd all come to watch her perform, and she realized that she couldn't wait to show them what she could do. The chairs – taking up all of the other floor area – were full of people from the town, and there were lots of other people's parents and friends there. But the only ones she wanted to impress were her own and, in that moment, suddenly everything seemed easier. It didn't really matter what Sam thought. Tara was here to perform for her family and friends, and that was what she was going to do.

The music started, and she focused on the routine. She knew now that it didn't matter if she didn't do things absolutely perfectly. It wasn't a competition and there were no judges to say she wasn't good enough. The group performed most of the routine together, but there were also moments when they performed balances in the pairs or groups they usually worked in. Tara and Lindsay performed all their balances well – including standing on shoulders, and counterbalance, where Tara stood on Lindsay's thighs and they held hands, leaning as far away from each other as they could. And she felt perfectly in time with everyone else in the sections where the whole group did the same steps and moves. It was tempting to look for Mum and Dad's reaction to some of the skills she'd learned, but she didn't want to lose concentration.

The trickiest section was near the end of the

routine. The pairs and trio and the group of four boys all performed a different balance at the same time. Tara and Lindsay had been working on their favourite balance – where Lindsay held Tara in a handstand on her thigh – and Tara could now move her legs from a straight handstand into the splits, upside down. While she held the position, Tara imagined the looks on Kate and Emily's faces. She brought her legs back up to a handstand before twisting them to one side to come down neatly to the floor. Lindsay stood up and a fraction of a second later, the entire group – who had all come down from their balances at the same time – bounced forward into handsprings. Tara landed hers more neatly than she'd ever managed before, stretched and grinned widely at Dad. A few more dance steps and jumps and it was all over. They finished in a group in the middle of the floor and everyone threw one arm up towards the ceiling on the last note of the music.

The sound of the audience clapping was much

louder than it had been in Kate's back garden. Of course, Tara remembered, there were a lot more people here! The gymnasts posed as a group while someone took a photo for the lobby wall. Tara smiled at her friends, gave Anna a tiny wave, then followed Lindsay and the others back out into the lobby.

She couldn't stop smiling. That was the most fun she'd ever had in her life! She grabbed Lindsay's arm and started jumping up and down with her.

"Amazing! Brilliant!" she sang.

Lindsay laughed. "You're going to be addicted to this, I can tell," she said.

"Wasn't that great?" Tara babbled to anyone standing nearby.

"It certainly was," said a familiar voice behind her. Tara spun around. "Well done, everyone," said Clare, who had been watching from the edge of the audience. "Silverdale should be very proud to have all of you."

Tara smiled to herself as Clare went back in to watch the rest of the display. Tara and the others went back to the changing room to get their things.

"I bet the handspring bit looked really cool," said Tara.

"I saw your landing," said Jasmine. "Better than ever!"

"Yep!" Tara grinned at her.

"You did alright," Sam admitted. Tara couldn't help smiling at that. Of course it was too much to hope that Sam might think she was actually *good*, but she didn't mind, really. She'd done the very best she could do, and that was enough for her friends and family.

The gymnasts crept in behind the audience to watch the last few routines. When Tara found her friends at the end of the display, Emily and Kate pounced on her immediately and hugged her tightly.

"That was *so* good!" cried Kate.

"I knew you'd be amazing, and you were!" said Emily.

"Did you really think so? You're not just saying that?" asked Tara.

"We definitely, completely, really thought so," said Kate, finally letting her out of the hug. Straight away she was grabbed by Mum for another hug.

"You were great, darling," she said.

"I never thought I'd see my little Tara in that display," said Dad. Tara cringed at the word "little" but then grinned at Dad.

"Tara, you're the best gymnast ever," Anna said proudly.

When Tara went to bed that night, after everyone had talked on and on about how great the whole display had been, she closed her eyes and pictured the group of acrobatic gymnasts she'd seen on TV. She imagined herself in the place of one of the gymnasts at the top of the balances – after the display, she could guess what it would feel like to perform such spectacular things.

The best bit, though, was being part of a group – working together and knowing that her own gymnastics skills and balances were part of a bigger routine that looked amazing when it was all put together. She remembered walking out onto the floor and thought that the audience probably didn't notice that she was any different to the rest of the group. And she wasn't, she realized. She was a Silverdale gymnast, too, just like Jasmine and Sophie. She'd be in a photo on the wall in the lobby soon, and maybe at next year's summer camp, someone would look at it and wish to be like her.

She wondered if she'd ever be in one of the competition photos with a medal or a trophy. At that moment, anything seemed possible. Next week, she would go back to the gym and they'd get to work on learning new skills, new balances. She would learn to do a backflip and a front somersault. After that, she had no idea what would come next – but she couldn't wait to find out. She drifted off to sleep, thinking of everything else she wanted to learn. And in her dreams that night, she performed her first full-twisting somersault.

There are lots of different **gym moves**. Here are some of the moves that Tara and Lindsay learn. They work together in Acro Gymnastics as a pair. Lindsay is the **base** so she lifts and holds Tara, who is the **top**, in different balances.

Backflip: a move where Tara swings her arms back and pushes off with her feet. She lands on her hands with her body arched then flips her legs up and over her head, then she pushes off with her hands to land back on both feet.

Backward walkover: Tara bends over backwards from a standing position with one leg raised until her hands reach the floor and her body forms an arch. Her legs then kick over, passing through the splits, to land standing up again.

Balance: *where Tara holds a fixed pose with Lindsay.*

Counter-balance: *Lindsay stands with her knees bent and feet apart. Tara stands on Lindsay's thighs, facing her. They grip each other's wrists, both then lean back until their arms are straight.*

Front somersault: *Tara turns head over heels in the air in a tucked shape to land back on her feet.*

Handspring: *a move where Tara lunges into a handstand, then flips over onto her feet.*

Round-off: *a fast cartwheel which Tara springs out of and lands on two feet.*

Standing front angel: Lindsay stands up straight and holds Tara above her head. Tara balances horizontally in a T shape with Lindsay's hands on her hips.

Standing on shoulders balance: Tara stands with one foot on each of Lindsay's shoulders while Lindsay holds onto her calves. They can do this with Lindsay kneeling down, kneeling up with one foot on the floor, or standing.

Straddle: in this position Tara sits on the floor with her legs out wide making a right angle.

Straddle lever balance: Tara balances on her hands with her legs held in the straddle position.

Y-balance: *standing on one leg, Tara holds her other foot with her hand and stretches her leg out to the side, so that her body forms a Y shape.*

Q and A session with
Jane Lawes

Why did you write Gym Stars?

My sister and I loved gymnastics when we were younger, but our local library only had one very old series about it. When I started writing Summertime and Somersaults, I just tried to write the book that I would have wanted to read. I absolutely loved writing Gym Stars, and hope you enjoy them too!

When did you start doing gym?

I'd always enjoyed doing cartwheels and handstands in PE lessons at school, but I think I was about ten or eleven – the same age as Tara – when I started to practise in the garden all the time.

Who is your favourite gymnast?

I admire Beth Tweddle because she did so much to lead Team GB and bring the sport into the spotlight, but my favourite gymnast who'll be competing in Rio is Claudia Fragapane – she's so powerful and her floor routines are fantastic. Plus, she's small like me!

Who is your favourite Acro Gymnastics group?

Spelbound, who won Britain's Got Talent in 2010, went to the same gym club as me – they're great!

What is your favourite gymnastics move?

I always loved doing backward walkovers because I worked so hard to learn how to do them, and once I could it felt great! Somersaults are fun, too, and they look amazing when champion gymnasts perform them with twists.

What is your gymnastics top tip?

Gymnastics moves can take a long time to learn, so don't be disappointed if you can't do something straight away – keep practising and you'll get there! Gymnastics is a lot of fun, so enjoy it!

Tara's Gym Star dreams

continue in these dazzling titles:

ISBN: 9781474922944

ISBN: 9781474922951

Also by Jane Lawes:

Ballet Stars

Follow Tash's adventures at Aurora House,
the boarding ballet school where dancing
dreams come true!

ISBN: 9781409583530

ISBN: 9781409583547

ISBN: 9781409583554

Usborne Quicklinks

For links to websites where you can watch video clips of gymnastics routines and find out more about balances and basic skills and gymnastics organizations, go to the Usborne Quicklinks website at www.usborne.com/quicklinks and enter the keywords "gym stars".

Please read the internet safety guidelines displayed at the Usborne Quicklinks website.

For more dazzling reads head to
www.usborne.com/fiction